10 IDEAS TO SAVE THE PLANET

Giuseppe D'Anna

illustrated by
Clarissa Corradin

Starry
Forest
Books

CONTENTS

THE FIRST STEPS  p. 4

1. PROTECT THE BEES p. 6

2. USE LESS PLASTIC  p. 10

3. RECYCLE  p. 14

4. CONSUME LOCAL AND SEASONAL PRODUCE p. 18

5. CONSERVE ENERGY p. 22

6. WALK OR RIDE YOUR BIKE p. 26

7. REDUCE WASTE p. 30

8. CONSERVE WATER  p. 34

9. SAVE PAPER  p. 36

10. RESPECT WILD ANIMALS  p. 38

THE FIRST STEPS

Congratulations! By picking up this book, you're on your way to making a BIG difference.

Did you know our planet is suffering from pollution? Do you want to understand what is happening? Or do you want to find out what you—yes, you!—can do to help the planet get all the help it needs? If you are reading this, it's because you care about the planet. And caring about the planet is the first step in making change!

Every day, under our noses, pollution becomes more and more visible: paper thrown in the street, plastic littering the ocean, dark smoke rising from factories, and smelly fumes coming out of our cars. Many, many things (sometimes the most unnoticeable ones) damage the environment around us.

It's time to make a change. Are you ready?

You might be thinking, "But I don't own a factory! I don't even drive!" True. If you think only grown-ups can save the planet . . . think again!

YOU AND YOUR FRIENDS CAN DO IT TOO!

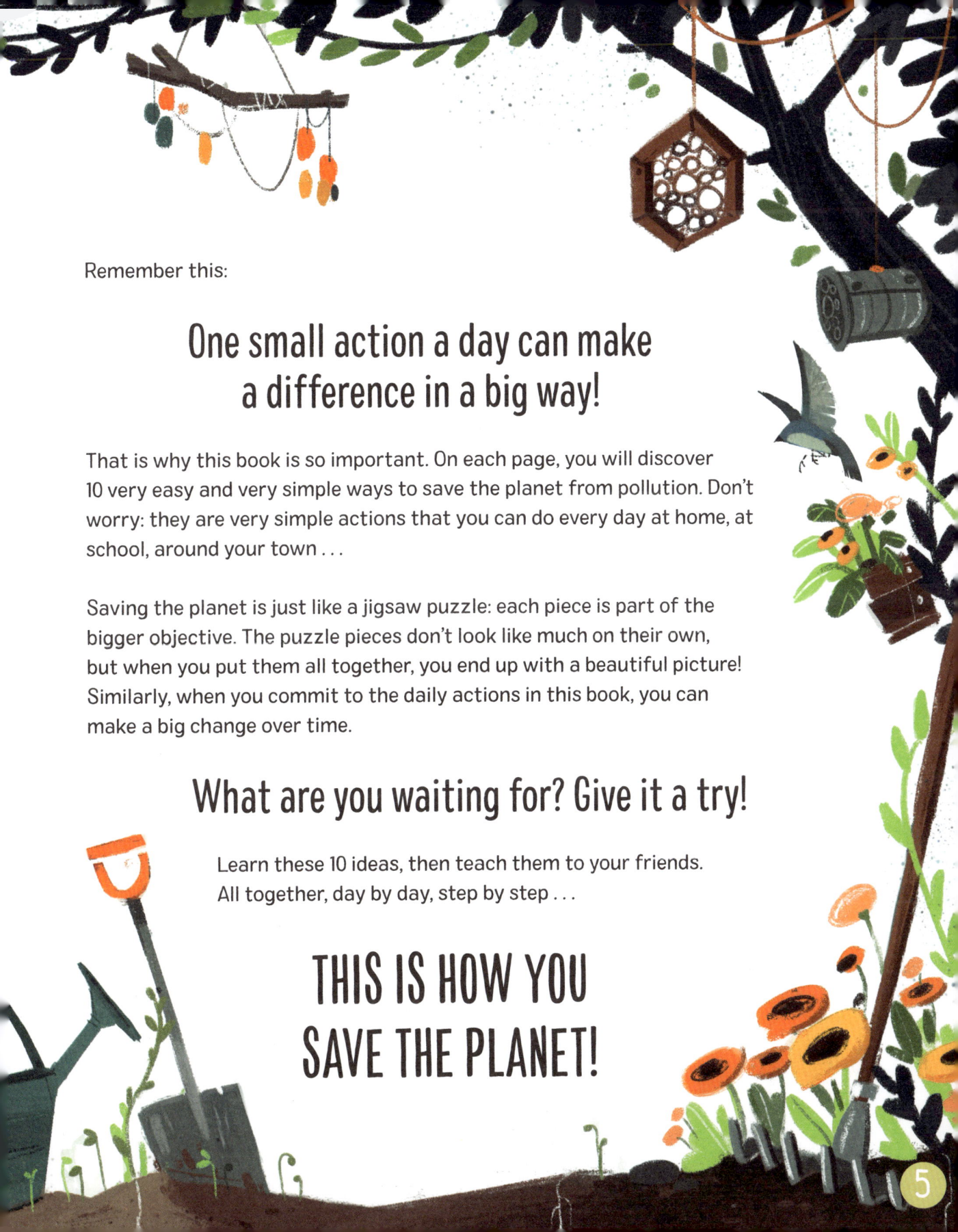

Remember this:

One small action a day can make a difference in a big way!

That is why this book is so important. On each page, you will discover 10 very easy and very simple ways to save the planet from pollution. Don't worry: they are very simple actions that you can do every day at home, at school, around your town . . .

Saving the planet is just like a jigsaw puzzle: each piece is part of the bigger objective. The puzzle pieces don't look like much on their own, but when you put them all together, you end up with a beautiful picture! Similarly, when you commit to the daily actions in this book, you can make a big change over time.

What are you waiting for? Give it a try!

Learn these 10 ideas, then teach them to your friends. All together, day by day, step by step . . .

THIS IS HOW YOU SAVE THE PLANET!

01 PROTECT THE BEES

Did you know that there are fewer and fewer bees in the world every day? Luckily, we can protect them by creating small (and fragrant) flowered oases for them.

How to Make a Bee-Saving Oasis

It's very easy. Find some flower seeds that are "**friends of the bees,**" i.e., their favorites. Bees love a lot of flowers and herbs whose seeds you can find at garden stores. Perhaps you know some of them already: thyme, rosemary, lavender, sunflower, poppy, marigold, mallow, dill, cumin, cilantro, fennel, clover, borage, melilot, and more! The bees are greedy for them!

Don't worry—you don't need to get all of them; the ones you do find will be more than enough!

Then, choose the right place to plant your seeds. If you are not able to find the right place to plant your seeds, no problem! Flowers in pots will be just fine, and you can place them anywhere you like—even on your balcony or windowsill, if you don't have a garden.

You can even do this at school, with the help of your teachers and your classmates (the more people, the better). Once you have permission, find a **nice area on campus and grab your shovel and watering can**! In many cities, you can even plant your own flowers in parks and other public spaces. Ask around to find out if you're allowed to do it.

Remember that flowers need water and sunlight in order to grow. And they are not the only ones . . . Always leave a bowl of water in your bee-saving oasis.

Those small, buzzing insects will thank you!

WHY PROTECT THE BEES?

Our busy bee friends are the perfect example of how someone very small can do something very big—just like you! Do you know why?

Bees help many plants reproduce.

Here's how it works: A little bee is attracted to the nectar inside a flower, and while it gorges itself on nectar, its legs get covered in pollen. When it moves on to another flower of the same species, that pollen comes off its legs and fertilizes the flower. Slowly, a fruit ripens, containing a seed that is ready to generate a new plant!

Basically, without bees, many living things would no longer exist: fruits, seeds, and most plants that are essential for animals and humans.

But bees are in danger! Pollution and pesticides used in agriculture threaten the bees: **their toxic components are harmful and kill more and more bees every day**. This is why creating your small bee-saving oasis is important; it is the first step in helping them multiply again!

DID YOU KNOW THAT…?

Bees have a big **stinger** they use when they feel threatened. However, bees use their stingers rarely because they die immediately after their stingers fall out! **Wasps**, on the other hand, can sting several times (that's why they are very dangerous!).

Bees and wasps look similar. They both have wings and black and yellow stripes. But it's easy to tell them apart: bees are chunky and fuzzy, while wasps are thin and smooth.

Steer clear of bee nests to keep the insects safe, and stay far away from wasp nests to keep yourself safe!

USE LESS PLASTIC

Plastic is everywhere: bottles, plates, bags. Learning to use less of it is easy. Here's how!

Ditch those disposable cups!

 How many times a day do you drink water from a plastic cup and then throw it away? Use a cup made of glass or hard plastic (which you can wash), and you will avoid wasting a lot of plastic. Easy! The same can be said for plates, utensils, and straws. Disposable objects are made to be used once and then thrown away. Many disposable objects contain plastic, which increases plastic consumption exponentially. This means it's best for the planet if you use them as little as possible!

If you aren't at home, here is a simple and fun solution:

Bring your own water bottle!

 There are lots to choose from; you can choose one that is your favorite color, or you can personalize it. Add your favorite stickers or write your name on it . . . then fill it with water or your favorite drinks as many times as you want!

How do you reduce plastic when you are at a party?
If there are disposable cups and plates, you can write your name on them with a marker so that you don't have to take a new one every time.

You can do a lot more to reduce plastic waste.
If you need a new pencil holder for your desk, you can make one by cutting a plastic bottle in half (with an adult's help), then coloring it and adding some decoration to it—like your favorite wrapping paper, a bow, or a sticker.

And what do you do when the ice cream carton is empty?
You can use the tub to hold objects: clean it, decorate it, then fill it with little items you misplace—like stickers, candy, tissue, and more.

WHY USE LESS PLASTIC?

The more plastic we use, the more we waste; it piles up into mountains that are discarded in some forgotten place on the planet.

Only a small amount of plastic litter is **recycled**. (If you don't know what recycling is, don't worry—we will talk about it later!) Plastic that is not recycled properly ends up in a few places: in **landfills** where it just piles up over time; in **incinerators** where it is burned and pollutes the air; or in **nature** where it threatens native wildlife. Plastic objects that litter the ground or the ocean do not decompose quickly or easily, which means they will stay there for a long time.

 **Do you know how much plastic ends up in the ocean each year?**

ABOUT 8 MILLION TONS!

All this litter has a tragic impact on the animals that live in the ocean and surrounding areas. For example, sea turtles mistake plastic bags for jellyfish, so they often eat them (and that's not good for their tummies at all!). The same happens with seagulls and other sea animals. This is the result of plastic being thrown away incorrectly.

Better to use less of it, right?

DID YOU KNOW THAT…?

Many countries are trying to be plastic-free by investing in alternative materials; these materials are **compostable**.

There are disposable plates that look like they are plastic but are actually made of sugarcane or bamboo. Instead of hanging around for hundreds of years after you throw them away, these plates transform into compost, which nourishes the same earth that generated the plants they were made from.

Yes, there are plates that are compostable too!

 # RECYCLE

Recycling means putting each piece of trash in the right bin.

You can learn to recognize different kinds of recyclables too!

 Food leftovers like pizza crusts, apple cores, and eggshells are called **organic waste**. Put these in the compost bin. You can put compostable plates and utensils in there too.

 Designate a bin for **paper** and **cardboard**, where you can throw old and used notebooks, newspapers that you no longer need, and some snack packages.

 Plastic (yogurt cups, detergent bottles, etc.) needs to be disposed of separately; the same with **glass**. Don't forget to recycle **steel** and **aluminum** (cans, tins, etc.) as well.

Lastly...

 There is **special waste** (batteries, printer cartridges, medicines, etc.) that must be disposed of properly. And there is general garbage, which doesn't belong to the previous categories and should be disposed of in the trash.

Now you are ready to start recycling!

Recycling rules differ from one state to another, so sometimes it's necessary to ask an adult for help. Now it's time to become a . . .

BLACK BELT IN RECYCLING!

WHY RECYCLE?

Simple. It allows us to do something very important: reuse waste.

The recycling truck collects the recycled waste and takes it to a plant; there, it is checked, sorted, and, if necessary, compressed or squeezed into smaller shapes to take up less space.

Then it is sent to a transformation center where it is turned into completely new objects. **Recycling lets us reuse discarded objects and avoid damaging the environment.**

All this is possible when you throw each object into the correct bin!

Unfortunately, the waste that is not recycled is a big problem because it pollutes for a very long time.
- A piece of chewing gum thrown on the ground stays there for **5 YEARS**.
- A soda can lasts for **100 YEARS**.
- A plastic bag can stick around for **1,000 YEARS**!

The best way to help the planet stay clean is to separate your trash and recycling.

 *DID YOU KNOW THAT…?*

Recycled waste can be turned into unexpected objects. For instance, **fleece**—a very soft fabric—comes from plastic. Yes, your hoodie might have come from plastic bottles! Recycled glass can be used to make **artificial grass** for soccer fields.

What about leftover food?
It becomes compost, which helps plants grow stronger.

04 CONSUME LOCAL AND SEASONAL PRODUCE

The fruit and vegetable section of the grocery store has everything year round: juicy oranges, fuzzy kiwis, eye-watering onions, and giant zucchini.

They may sit on the same shelves, but they have different stories! Some come from far away, some from around the corner. Some fruits and vegetables are **seasonal**, which ripen at the same time of year they are sold. Others are grown in greenhouses, which are special structures where plants can grow all year.

How do you tell them apart? Unfortunately, you can't "see" if the strawberries ripened under the sun or under **artificial lights**, which help them grow even when it's cold outside. So, it is better to learn (and remember!) which fruits and vegetables grow in each season of the year.

There's an easy and exciting way to do this...

 Get a piece of poster board, and, with a marker, draw four equal sections, one for each season: spring, summer, fall, and winter. With your teacher's or guardian's help, fill each area of the board by drawing and coloring the **fruits** and **vegetables** that grow where you live during each season.

Get creative and discover local produce!

 Once completed, keep the board in the kitchen, classroom, or your room. You can refer to the board to know what produce is best to eat based on the season you are in. If you accompany your parent or guardian (or even your babysitter!) to the grocery store, find **products that come from local farm producers**. Or visit a local farmers market!

If you're lucky, you might meet the farmer who grew the fruits and vegetables. Look how proud they are of their hard work!

WHY CONSUME LOCAL AND SEASONAL PRODUCE?

To stock stores with out-of-season fruits and vegetables, products need to be shipped in from other countries (hotter or colder countries, depending on the product), or they need to be grown in greenhouses, using special lighting and heating systems.

This inevitably pollutes the planet, but we can reduce it.

Imagine the journey that a zucchini makes, traveling all the way from another country to arrive on the supermarket shelf. It is loaded onto a truck with other vegetables, then a train, maybe even a ship too. All of these modes of transportation release carbon dioxide, a substance that is very harmful to the environment.

The longer the journey for our zucchini, the more polluted the air becomes!

In order to grow out-of-season fruits and vegetables, greenhouses use heating systems to keep the plants warm. These heating systems produce carbon dioxide—and a lot of it!

Forget strawberries in winter! Eat seasonal fruits, like apples, tangerines, or grapefruit, instead. Don't forget—you can always check your poster board!

DID YOU KNOW THAT…?

Produce that ripens in the sun contains more **vitamins** and **minerals** than produce ripened artificially. Produce that is sold out of season is removed from its nutritious soil before it is ripe and ripens on its journey. Produce grown in greenhouses also receives less sunlight than fruit cultivated outdoors. This means eating local and seasonal produce is good for your health too!

# CONSERVE ENERGY

Thanks to electricity, we enjoy a lot of comforts in our homes. The fridge keeps the food fresh, light bulbs give us light any time we want (with just a flick of the switch!), and the TV makes it quick and easy to watch our favorite shows with friends.

 **Did you know that by being a bit more careful, you can save energy without having to give anything up? It's true!**

The first rule is very simple, and it applies to almost everything (e.g., TV, computer, video game console): **When you aren't using something, turn it off.** If you are planning to reuse it soon, pause it.

Remember, technology still uses energy even when it's not in use. For example, when you're done with the TV, always remember to turn it off. Some remotes will have a red-light signal to remind you that the TV is still using up energy!

To avoid wasting energy, turn off appliances completely.

 **This rule applies to light bulbs too.** You should avoid keeping lights on when you don't need them and instead remember to turn them off every time you leave the room. If you come back to the room, it's not a big deal . . . **You can turn the lights back on with the flick of a switch!**

Before going out, check around the house with an adult for any appliances that need to be turned off. All clear!

There are special **energy-saving bulbs** that give off light by consuming as little energy as possible. Ask an adult if you already have these bulbs in your house. If not, suggest using them!

 **And the fridge?** You can't turn it off, or the food will rot. So keep in mind that the longer you leave the refrigerator open, the more energy it uses! Think about what you need from the fridge before you open it. Maintain its proper temperature and save energy too!

WHY CONSERVE ENERGY?

Almost all of the energy we use every day comes from **fossil fuels**, which are very rare (and expensive) resources that are burned to create energy. Fossil fuels also generate huge quantities of carbon dioxide (CO_2), the **#1 enemy of clean air**.

That's not all! The most common fuels are **coal**, **oil**, and **natural gas**, which are found deep underground. To extract them, huge, special machines are used to break the soil and dig deep into the ground. Then the fuels are transported to energy plants.

Each one of these operations is highly polluting, because several forms of transportation are involved. The result? More fumes and more carbon dioxide!

 It's a no-brainer: if everyone commits to being careful with energy, we will need less of it and, subsequently, have less demand for fossil fuels!

The best way to help the environment is to waste as little energy as possible.

DID YOU KNOW THAT...?

There is **clean energy**, which is produced without harmful emissions into the environment. Clean energy is still developing because there is still a lot of research to do. Maybe you'll help develop it!

These are the most popular sources of clean energy:

- **Solar energy** is obtained from mirror-like panels that absorb sunlight. These are often installed on house roofs.

- Have you seen the giant windmills that sometimes line the side of the highway? Those are called turbines. They capture **wind energy**.

- Hydroelectric generators turn the force of rivers, waterfalls, and sea currents into **hydraulic energy**.

06 WALK OR RIDE YOUR BIKE

 Towns and cities are often full of cars coming and going, like an army of angry ants. Cars' smelly fumes engulf the roads, while the sound of growling engines and trumpeting horns fill the air.

Although using the car is necessary sometimes, a nice walk or bicycle ride can be a great alternative to get to where you need to be!

When your destination is nearby, walk instead of driving.

It might take longer to get where you're going, but just think! **You might notice something new on your route.**

Perhaps there is a garden that you never noticed before or a statue that didn't look as beautiful when seen from the car window. And maybe you'll make a new friend—human or animal!

A walk outside can be full of pleasant surprises!

Of course, not all places you would like to go can be easily reached on foot.

 Maybe your school, your favorite park, or your best friend's house is not that close. If so, you can always ride your bicycle. Many towns have long cycling paths where you can ride safely, away from cars and pedestrians. **Be careful not to go too fast, and don't forget to always wear a helmet!**

 Buses, trains, and subways . . . oh my! If your destination is farther away or the weather is bad, **you can opt for public transportation**. An adult can help you learn how public transport in your area works and where it can take you.

NOW YOU ARE READY FOR NEW ADVENTURES!

 # WHY CHOOSE TO WALK OR RIDE YOUR BIKE?

Easy! Choosing to walk or ride your bike minimizes carbon-dioxide production.

Have you ever heard of greenhouse gas?

That is what happens when we produce **too much carbon dioxide**: when it reaches the atmosphere (i.e., the air that surrounds our planet), this gas absorbs **the warmth of the sun's rays** and **the temperature rises**, which causes **global warming**. A common result is that the seasons get mixed up. It can rain a lot or be very, very hot during periods of the year when we least expect it.

The consequences are often devastating, such as floods and sudden fires.

The trick to avoid motor transport is to find new ways to travel.

Cars, motorcycles, and buses produce exhaust fumes that accumulate and form smog, which harms the environment and people's health. There are great ways to avoid motor transportation entirely! For instance, there's the **"walking bus."** Instead of a vehicle, it is formed by children walking together (along with accompanying adults). **No more smelly fumes!**

DID YOU KNOW THAT…?

In 2018, a 15-year-old Swedish girl took to the streets and asked her government to commit to reducing carbon-dioxide emissions. Her name is **Greta Thunberg**. Greta started by organizing strikes every Friday in front of Sweden's parliament building. Now, she travels the globe calling attention to climate change! Her determination has led to the "**Fridays for Future**" movement.

Anybody can make the same effort as Greta to stop pollution.

 The actions in this book are a great way to start!

07 REDUCE WASTE

Do you know how much waste each human being produces every day? **More than 2 pounds (1 kilo)!** It is a national average, which means that some countries produce more of it, others less.

 If each one of us made the best and full use of what we have, waste would definitely decrease.

Doing your part is easy.

Soap, shampoo, conditioner . . . use the right quantity. A bit of foam and a few bubbles are enough to wash yourself properly.

Have you ever thought about giving away the clothes that no longer fit you or the games you don't play with anymore? If they are still in good condition, **you can donate them**! Perhaps you have a younger sibling, cousin, or friend who can use them. You can also receive things from someone older than you.

Old or worn-out objects can be turned into something else.

You've already read about it in this book, when talking about plastic. Remember?

For example, **mismatched socks** can become funny puppets. You just need to draw a face on them or sew on a couple of buttons as eyes. Don't forget to ask your parents or another adult for help! Then slip your hand inside, and you're ready for the show!

USE YOUR IMAGINATION TO REUSE EVERYTHING YOU CAN.

WHY REDUCE WASTE?

Factories generate carbon dioxide when the machines are at work, like cars do, but factories produce much, much more of it! Some of them don't even stop at night or on the weekend.

That's not all!

Do you remember the example of the zucchini, harming the environment by traveling on trucks, trains, and ships? Products that are made and ready to be sold are transported to different stores in the same way. **The more we buy, the more we must produce and transport.**

By reducing waste and reusing old things, we don't need so many new things to be made, which limits the carbon dioxide we produce!

DID YOU KNOW THAT...?

If you don't know anyone to pass your unused things to, you can donate them to local groups that help the less fortunate. These groups accept donations of **clothes, books, toys, notebooks, and more for those in need**.

 With the help of an adult, look up what donation centers are near you! Prepare a box or bag of items to donate—on your own or with friends!

We can help the planet and lend a hand to other children too. Easy!

CONSERVE WATER

Water is precious. It flows so fast from the faucet that it is very tricky to understand how much we use, don't you think? But it's still possible to conserve!

 Always turn the faucet off while you brush your teeth. It is important to brush them well, but it's not necessary to keep the water running while you do it. You can turn the water back on when it's time to rinse your mouth and clean your toothbrush. A gleaming smile without wasting a single unnecessary drop of water!

Try taking more showers and fewer baths. It takes a lot of water to fill a bathtub. **Showering is a great way to conserve water—and time!** Just enough for a quick shampoo and a good rinse!

Keep the water running only when needed.

 # WHY CONSERVE WATER?

Water is a **renewable resource**, which means it gets generated continuously. You can see this in the water cycle: Water on the ground evaporates up into the air, then falls to the ground as precipitation, like rain or snow. And repeat!

However, water is also a limited resource because it's not available in infinite amounts. This is because the **groundwater layers** (i.e., the underground deposits that the water gets extracted from) need time to fill up again. This is why, if we use too much, we risk being left without it.

Running water is a great luxury, but it's not accessible in some parts of the world.

For example, East Africa has a limited supply of water because of drought. On the other hand, the Democratic Republic of the Congo's water resources make up 50 percent of the African continent's water reserves. However, it is difficult for people in the country's rural areas to get access to water because of limited water sanitation and transportation systems.

09 SAVE PAPER

Writing, drawing, decorating, wrapping... while you can use paper in many ways, it's also important to use every inch of it efficiently!

 Sheets of paper have two sides, so why not use both?
Don't use a new sheet of paper if you don't need to! Flip over the page you just used and start another masterpiece.

 What can you do with old newspapers and magazines?
Apart from paper airplanes, they can be turned into nice decorations and special garlands for a party. Here's how: Take a pair of round-tipped scissors and cut out many strips of paper. Attach the two ends of a strip with a stapler and form a ring. Then thread another strip of paper through the ring, and staple the two ends again... Repeat until the chain of rings is as long as you'd like!

Quick and fun.

The result?

A UNIQUE GARLAND!

WHY SAVE PAPER?

Paper is made from trees, so the more paper you **recycle**, the fewer trees that need to be cut down. It is essential to **protect trees**, because the process of **photosynthesis** produces the oxygen all organisms need to breathe. At the same time, it cleans the air of excess carbon dioxide.

But that's not all . . . Their roots make the ground stable, preventing landslides and floods.

That's why many organizations are committing to planting as many trees as possible in green areas around towns and cities. Find out with your parents or guardians if your community offers the opportunity to . . .

GROW YOUR OWN TREE!

10 RESPECT WILD ANIMALS

When you take a walk outside in nature, you might bump into **wild animals** (i.e., animals that live freely in nature). Here are some little rules that you can follow to respect them and their habitats.

Never touch the babies.

 It's common to want to cuddle a cute baby animal, but you never should. Touching a baby animal can put them at risk: Moms in the wild recognize their little ones by smell. If your scent covers the baby animal's scent, the mother may not recognize them and might abandon their baby.

Never capture them.

 Unlike pets and other domestic animals, wild animals are not used to being touched or put in a carrier. Even if you want to observe a critter more closely, you will likely hurt them—and you will definitely scare them. It's best to leave wild creatures alone in their natural habitats.

Respect their homes.

 Nests, burrows, anthills . . . discovering them is exciting, but remember this: They may look like holes in the ground (or simple woven twigs), but they are real homes for wild animals. If you find one, observe it from a distance with a pair of binoculars!

Never feed them.

 Giving part of your snack to a furry or feathered friend may feel like a kind gesture, but it can lead to unpleasant consequences. Human food will give a little fox a stomachache. It is also important for cubs to learn how to get their food themselves. If they get used to being fed by humans, surviving in nature will be challenging for them.

Observing wild animals from a distance—without touching, feeding, or moving them— is the best way to help them live free and happy!

GIUSEPPE D'ANNA

Giuseppe was born and raised in sunny Sicily and trained to be a graphic designer and artist in the hills of Tuscany. He currently lives here and there (as well as sometimes everywhere) and occasionally finds his fun writing books for children and young adults.

CLARISSA CORRADIN

Clarissa was born in Ivrea, Italy, in 1992. She attended the Albertina Academy of Fine Arts in Turin, where she studied painting and illustration. Now she passionately illustrates children's books, including White Star Kids' *Avery Everywhere* series.

White Star Kids® is a registered trademark property of
White Star s.r.l.
© 2020 White Star s.r.l.
Piazzale Luigi Cadorna, 6
20123 Milan, Italy
www.whitestar.it

Starry Forest® is a registered trademark of
Starry Forest Books, Inc.
This 2021 edition published by Starry Forest Books, Inc.
P.O. Box 1797, 217 East 70th Street, New York, NY 10021

All rights reserved. No part of this publication may be reproduced, stored in a retrieval system, or transmitted in any form or by any means (including electronic, mechanical, photocopying, recording, or otherwise) without prior written permission from the publisher.

ISBN 978-1-951784-04-1

Manufactured in Romania

2 4 6 8 10 9 7 5 3 1

03/21